HOPSCOTCH ADVENTURES

Robin and the Knight

Tales of Robin Hood

First published in 2006 by
Franklin Watts
338 Euston Road
London
NW1 3BH

Franklin Watts Australia
Hachette Children's Books
Level 17/207 Kent Street
Sydney
NSW 2000

A CIP catalogue record for this book is available
from the British Library.

ISBN (10) 0 7496 6686 2 (hbk)
ISBN (13) 978-0-7496-6686-6 (hbk)
ISBN (10) 0 7496 6699 4 (pbk)
ISBN (13) 978-0-7496-6699-6 (pbk)

Series Editor: Jackie Hamley
Series Advisor: Dr Barrie Wade
Series Designer: Peter Scoulding

Printed in China

Franklin Watts is a division of
Hachette Children's Books.

HOPSCOTCH ADVENTURES

Robin and the Knight

by Damian Harvey and Martin Remphry

W
FRANKLIN WATTS
LONDON•SYDNEY

Robin Hood and Little John
were hiding by the road, hoping
a rich knight or a greedy
bishop might pass by.

"I can hear someone," said Robin.
"It looks like a rich, lazy knight,"
said Little John. "Let's take his
money to give to the poor."

But as he rode closer, Robin and Little John could see the knight's clothes were torn and dirty.

"Welcome to Sherwood Forest," said Robin. "Friar Tuck is preparing a feast. I'd be pleased if you'd eat with me and my merry men tonight."

"Thank you," said the knight.
"I am Sir Richard."
"I had hoped for more than your thanks," said Robin.

"I see," said Sir Richard, "but ten
silver pennies are all I have."

"Why does a noble knight only have
ten silver pennies?" asked Robin.

"It is a sad tale," said Sir Richard. "My son was in a jousting <u>tournament</u>, and he beat many great knights."

"All was well until the final joust against Sir Walter. Their lances broke and Sir Walter was accidentally killed.

"My son was arrested and thrown
into jail. He would have died if I
had not paid his ransom."

"I used all my gold to set him free, and still had to borrow four hundred gold coins from the Abbot of St Mary's."

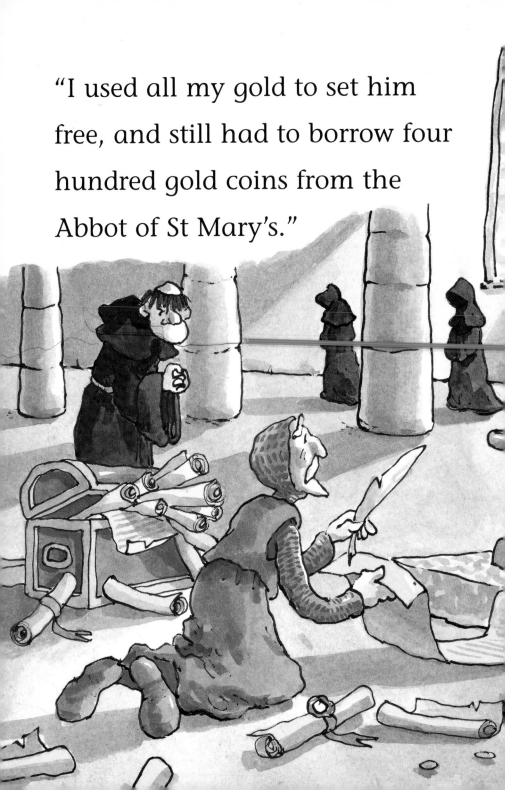

"Now, unless I repay the Abbot in three days, my castle and land will belong to him."

"Four hundred gold coins for your castle and land!" cried Robin Hood. "That Abbot is too greedy."

Robin Hood sent Will Scarlet to
count out four hundred gold coins
from their secret treasure store.

21

Robin gave the money to Sir Richard.

"Take this as a loan," he said.

"You can pay your debt to the

Abbot and repay me when you can."

Sir Richard went straight
to see the Abbot.

"Here are your four hundred gold coins," said Sir Richard. "Now keep your hands off my home!"

Next day, Robin and Little John
were walking by the road.
"I wish we could teach that greedy
Abbot a lesson," said Robin.

"Perhaps we can," said Little John.

"Here comes one of his monks."

"Welcome!" said Robin.

"Will you join us for a feast?"

"No!" said the monk.

"I have no money."

"If you have no money," said
Little John, "these four hundred
gold coins must be ours."

"There," said Robin.
"Our pockets are full again,
and Sir Richard doesn't have
to pay back his loan."

"But my stomach is still empty," said Little John.

"Come on," said Robin.

"We have a feast waiting!"

Hopscotch has been specially designed to fit the requirements of the National Literacy Strategy. It offers real books by top authors and illustrators for children developing their reading skills. There are 37 Hopscotch stories to choose from:

Marvin, the Blue Pig
ISBN 0 7496 4619 5

Plip and Plop
ISBN 0 7496 4620 9

The Queen's Dragon
ISBN 0 7496 4618 7

Flora McQuack
ISBN 0 7496 4621 7

Willie the Whale
ISBN 0 7496 4623 3

Naughty Nancy
ISBN 0 7496 4622 5

Run!
ISBN 0 7496 4705 1

The Playground Snake
ISBN 0 7496 4706 X

"Sausages!"
ISBN 0 7496 4707 8

The Truth about Hansel and Gretel
ISBN 0 7496 4708 6

Pippin's Big Jump
ISBN 0 7496 4710 8

Whose Birthday Is It?
ISBN 0 7496 4709 4

The Princess and the Frog
ISBN 0 7496 5129 6

Flynn Flies High
ISBN 0 7496 5130 X

Clever Cat
ISBN 0 7496 5131 8

Moo!
ISBN 0 7496 5332 9

Izzie's Idea
ISBN 0 7496 5334 5

Roly-poly Rice Ball
ISBN 0 7496 5333 7

I Can't Stand It!
ISBN 0 7496 5765 0

Cockerel's Big Egg
ISBN 0 7496 5767 7

How to Teach a Dragon Manners
ISBN 0 7496 5873 8

The Truth about those Billy Goats
ISBN 0 7496 5766 9

Marlowe's Mum and the Tree House
ISBN 0 7496 5874 6

Bear in Town
ISBN 0 7496 5875 4

The Best Den Ever
ISBN 0 7496 5876 2

ADVENTURE STORIES

Aladdin and the Lamp
ISBN 0 7496 6678 1 *
ISBN 0 7496 6692 7

Blackbeard the Pirate
ISBN 0 7496 6676 5 *
ISBN 0 7496 6690 0

George and the Dragon
ISBN 0 7496 6677 3 *
ISBN 0 7496 6691 9

Jack the Giant-Killer
ISBN 0 7496 6680 3 *
ISBN 0 7496 6693 5

TALES OF KING ARTHUR

1. The Sword in the Stone
ISBN 0 7496 6681 1 *
ISBN 0 7496 6694 3

2. Arthur the King
ISBN 0 7496 6683 8 *
ISBN 0 7496 6695 1

3. The Round Table
ISBN 0 7496 6684 6 *
ISBN 0 7496 6697 8

4. Sir Lancelot and the Ice Castle
ISBN 0 7496 6685 4 *
ISBN 0 7496 6698 6

TALES OF ROBIN HOOD

Robin and the Knight
ISBN 0 7496 6686 2 *
ISBN 0 7496 6699 4

Robin and the Monk
ISBN 0 7496 6687 0 *
ISBN 0 7496 6700 1

Robin and the Friar
ISBN 0 7496 6688 9 *
ISBN 0 7496 6702 8

Robin and the Silver Arrow
ISBN 0 7496 6689 7 *
ISBN 0 7496 6703 6

* hardback